Happy Boo Day

by Marcia Thornton Jones
and
Debbie Dadey

illustrated by John Steven Gurney

A
LITTLE APPLE
PAPERBACK

SCHOLASTIC INC.
New York   Toronto   London   Auckland   Sydney
Mexico City   New Delhi   Hong Kong

ISBN 0-439-15009-4

12 11 10 9 8 7 6 5 4 3 2 1   0 1 2 3 4 5/0

Printed in the U.S.A.   40

First Scholastic printing, February 2000

For my good friends
Gail, Bob, Lindsey, and Stacey Stoltz — DD

To Becky North, a great writer with
a treasure chest full of stories! — MTJ

Contents

1

Boo

"There's nothing to do," Ben complained. It was Saturday morning and Ben was sitting in the tree house with his sister, Annie, and their friend Jane.

"We could clean up this place," Annie suggested as she scooped a pile of Ben's old math papers into a corner.

"Cleaning is not my idea of fun," Jane admitted.

Ben sat up and snapped his fingers. "I've got it," he said. "What we need is a good game of soccer."

"It's no fun with just three people," Jane told him.

"No problem," Ben said. "We'll get Kilmer."

Before the girls could say "boo," Ben scrambled down from the tree house and was halfway next door to Hauntly Manor Inn. The girls had to hurry to catch up.

Ben, Annie, and Jane hopped up the warped steps and pounded on Kilmer's wooden door. Heavy footsteps echoed from within and the door slowly creaked open. Boris Hauntly looked down and smiled. The kids couldn't help but notice Boris' pointy eyeteeth. The long cape he always wore made him look like Dracula's twin brother.

"What a pleasure," Kilmer's father said in his thick Transylvanian accent. "Please come in."

The three kids stepped into the shadows of Hauntly Manor Inn. Kilmer's mother, Hilda, stood at the top of the curving staircase and smiled. "More visitors?" she asked. "What a nice surprise!" As usual, Hilda's hair stood straight up and she wore a lab coat with strange red, green, and purple stains on the front. Hilda was a scientist at F.A.T.S., the Federal Aeronautics Technology Station, and the kids suspected that she worked on

dangerous concoctions in her secret laboratory.

"We came to see Kilmer," Jane said. "Is he home?"

"I will get the birthday boy," Hilda called down to them before disappearing from sight.

"It's Kilmer's birthday?" Annie asked.

"Not until tomorrow," Boris told them. "I am in the middle of making his devil's food birthday cake. I must hurry back to the kitchen. Please make yourselves comfortable."

Boris left the kids standing in the living room and flew through the swinging door leading to the kitchen. Annie, Ben, and Jane perched on the end of the red velvet couch. Annie kept her legs straight out in front of her. She was sure she'd seen the giant claw feet on the couch moving once before.

Ben pointed to the corner where three huge spiders were busy weaving a giant web. "I wonder if Hilda ever gets Winifred's,

Elvira's, and Minerva's sticky webs caught in her hair," he said.

The kids were used to seeing Kilmer's three pet spiders hanging around Hauntly Manor, but they weren't used to seeing the spiders act like *this*.

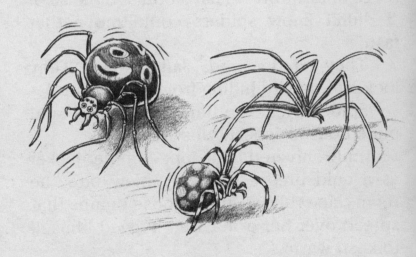

2
Fear Nothing

All three spiders suddenly dropped from their webs and scurried under a heavy piece of furniture. "That's odd," Annie said. "I didn't know spiders could move that fast."

"They acted scared," Jane added. "They look like they're hiding from something."

"Spiders fear nothing," Ben said and puffed out his chest. "Just like me."

Annie shivered and zipped up her jacket as a cold breeze suddenly blew into the room. Jane rubbed at the goose bumps that spread over her arms. Ben hugged himself to keep warm.

"It feels like dead fingers just grabbed my ankles," Jane yelped.

"The claw feet on the couch have come to life!" Annie screamed.

Ben, Annie, and Jane jumped up from the couch and huddled in the middle of the Hauntlys' living room.

Annie's eyes were squeezed shut. "Are they coming to get us?" she asked with a trembling voice.

Ben squinted at the dark wooden legs sticking out from under the couch. He bent down for a better look. "I don't think so," he said. "The claws aren't moving."

"Then what's causing that breeze?" Annie asked through chattering teeth. A definite chill had entered the living room.

"And what's that noise?" Jane asked. The kids stood still and listened. Heavy thumps moved across the creaking wooden floor of the living room. They sounded exactly like footsteps, but no one was there.

"We must be hearing things," Ben told the girls.

Annie peeked around the room and nodded. "It's just the house creaking," she said. "After all, the rest of Hauntly Manor Inn looks like it's falling apart."

8

That was true. The inn wasn't really old, but ever since the Hauntlys moved in and opened their bed-and-breakfast, the house at 13 Dedman Street had looked like it was ready to fall down. Shingles had flown off the roof and part of the railing around the front porch had collapsed into the yard. The grass and all the trees were brown. It didn't look much better on the inside, especially with Minerva's, Elvira's, and Winifred's silky webs draped in every corner and a heavy layer of dust covering the furniture.

"The floorboards are probably loose," Jane suggested, but her voice trembled when she said it.

The thumping continued across the room. It stopped as suddenly as it had begun.

"There," Jane said with a sigh. "It was nothing at all."

The words were barely out of her mouth when the door leading out of the living room swung open. Without a sound, the door clicked shut.

The three kids gulped. No one was there!

3
Ghostly Cruise

"It was only the wind," Ben whispered.

"I don't think so," Jane said slowly. "It sounded more like a ghost to me."

"A ghost?" Annie squealed.

Jane nodded, but before she could say anything else a loud booming sound came from outside the living room.

"Then it must be a ghost with combat boots," Annie moaned.

"That's just Kilmer," Ben said, rolling his eyes at his little sister.

Kilmer stomped into the room. Kilmer was in fourth grade just like Ben and Jane, but he was much taller than any other fourth-grader. Kilmer's hair was cut flat across the top, which made him look like Frankenstein's monster.

"Hello," Kilmer greeted them. "I can't

wait for you to meet my great-grandfather. He just floated over the ocean from Europe for my birthday."

"I've always wondered what a cruise ship would be like," Annie said. "I'll ask your great-grandfather."

"My great-grandfather has been just about everywhere," Kilmer told his friends.

"But there's no place like home," a tall, pale man dressed in white said as he entered the room. "The best place in the world is Hauntly Castle with all my ancestors. But the second best place is here at Hauntly Manor Inn."

Kilmer clapped his hands. "Great-grandfather, I want to introduce you to my best friends. This is Ben, Annie, and Jane."

"Please call me Franklin," Kilmer's great-grandfather said. "It is my great pleasure to meet you." His voice was so quiet he was practically whispering.

The kids took turns shaking hands with Kilmer's great-grandfather. Jane couldn't help noticing how cold Franklin's hands

were. Annie marveled at his solid white hair and mustache. Ben got a kick out of Franklin's old-fashioned clothes and shoes.

"How about some delicious treats?" Boris asked as he and Hilda pushed through the kitchen's swinging door. Boris carried a big silver tray, loaded with unusual-looking snacks.

"Please try some liver pâté and roasted pig snouts," Hilda offered.

"Thank you," Annie said politely, pretending to take a small nibble before putting it on a little black plate. Ben and Jane took small pieces and pretended to eat them, too. Boris was famous for making unusual treats. The kids were never brave enough to actually try them. Kilmer popped three of the roasted pig snouts into his mouth in one bite. Jane noticed that Franklin didn't eat any of the treats, either.

Franklin sat on a faded chair beside the couch. With his white hair and white clothes, he almost blended into the pale chair. It was hard to tell where the chair ended and Kilmer's great-grandfather began.

"How was your cruise to America, sir?" Annie asked Franklin.

Franklin frowned. "I will never take another one. When we hit that iceberg I thought it was the end of the world."

"Iceberg?" Ben asked. "That sounds scary."

Franklin nodded. "Oh, it was. And to think, that boat was supposed to be unsinkable. Instead of unsinkable, it did the unthinkable! People scrambled for lifeboats, but there weren't enough to save everyone. Through it all, the band played on."

"Hey," Ben said, "I've heard this story before."

"Shhh," Annie said. "I want to hear how Franklin got off the boat."

"When the ship started going down in that freezing water," Franklin continued, "I knew if I didn't keep my wits about me it would be the end of my life. It nearly was. Instead, it was the day my new life began!"

4

Titanic

"Franklin was on the *Titanic*!" Ben shouted after they left the Hauntlys'. They were standing on the cracked sidewalk in front of the Hauntlys' porch.

"Don't be crazy," Annie said. "Hardly anyone survived the *Titanic*."

Jane started to speak, but she was interrupted by a strange moaning sound.

Annie gulped. "What was that?"

Ben looked up into the dead tree branches. "It was just the wind," he said.

As if to answer Ben, the moaning sounded again. "That's not coming from the trees," Jane said nervously. "It's coming from the Hauntlys' attic."

"We should tell Kilmer," Annie said. "There could be something wrong up there."

"No," Jane said firmly, pulling Ben and Annie beside a dead bush for privacy. "I have a strange feeling about Kilmer's great-grandfather."

Jane paused to make sure no one else was around. She took a deep breath and told them, "I think Franklin is a ghost."

Ben laughed. "You're nuts," he said.

Jane stomped her foot. "I am not. You're the one who said he was on the *Titanic*. I think he died on the *Titanic* and became a ghost. That's what he meant when he said his new life began the day the *Titanic* sank."

Annie patted Jane on the back. "Kilmer's great-grandfather is old," Annie said, "but that doesn't make him a ghost."

"What about that cold breeze, the moaning, and the way the door swung open all by itself? Don't you think that's weird?" Jane asked. "And don't forget about the footsteps without a body attached!"

Annie nodded slowly. "He is very pale, and his skin is so cold."

"That doesn't make you a ghost or I'd be one every winter," Ben argued.

"But when Franklin sat in that chair it was almost like you could see right through him. And . . . he was on the *Titanic*," Jane said.

"That doesn't mean a thing. Lots of people survived the *Titanic* shipwreck," Ben said. "Let's forget all this ghost stuff and play soccer. We can play without Kilmer."

Just then, the door to Hauntly Manor Inn creaked open. The kids stared at the door. "Is that Kilmer?" Annie asked. "Maybe he can play after all."

"There's no one there," Jane whispered.

Annie grabbed Jane's arm. "It sounds like someone is walking down the steps, but I don't see anyone."

Jane nodded and looked at Ben. "I hope you're right about Kilmer's great-grandfather, or Kilmer's birthday will turn into a *boo* day."

5

Birthday Treat

"I can't believe I'm spending all my allowance on Kilmer," Ben complained. It was the next day and Jane, Ben, and Annie stood on the porch to Hauntly Manor Inn.

"Treating your best friend on his birthday is a great way to spend your allowance," Annie said as she pounded on the door to Hauntly Manor Inn.

Hilda opened the door and smiled at the three kids. "What a welcome surprise," she said. "Please come in. Kilmer and his great-grandfather are in the conservatory."

The kids knew a conservatory should be filled with plants, but the Hauntlys' conservatory was filled with pots of dirt and dead twigs. Kilmer sat on a mound of dirt, and his great-grandfather sat in the corner. He blended into the shadows so well that the kids almost didn't see him there.

"We want to treat you on your birthday," Jane said as soon as she saw Kilmer.

"We're taking you for a Doodlegum Shake!" Ben said.

Kilmer jumped up and licked his lips. "Doodlegum Shakes are better than anything I've ever tasted," he explained to his great-grandfather.

Annie nodded. "They're cold and sweet and thick and creamy!"

Franklin's eyes sparkled. "Mmmmmmm," he moaned as he rubbed his stomach. "A Doodlegum Shake sounds like the perfect treat for Kilmer's birthday," he said with a smile. "Have a wonderful time."

"I've been waiting for this all day," Ben said as the kids headed down Dedman Street toward Burger Doodle.

They had just turned the corner when Annie noticed a cold breeze. She zipped up her coat and shivered. "Do you think it's too cold for milk shakes?" she asked.

Ben shook his head. "It's never too cold for a milk shake," he told his sister.

Jane pulled her coat tight and opened her mouth to say something, but all of a sudden a dozen birds swooped out of a tree. Annie jumped and Jane let out a scream.

"I wonder what got their feathers ruffled," Ben said.

Kilmer shrugged. "Birds are flighty animals," he told his friends. "I never pay any attention to them."

Ben and Annie nodded, but Jane couldn't help noticing more birds scattering from the trees on their way to Burger Doodle.

But birds were the furthest thing from Jane's mind as they all ordered extra-large Doodlegum Shakes. They had just sat near a window and started sipping their shakes when a girl named Carey marched up to the front door. She led her huge Great Dane by a leash. The kids knew Carey's dog Chewy. He was famous for eating their soccer balls.

But Chewy wasn't interested in biting soccer balls today.

Chewy looked straight through the window at the kids and barked from deep inside his chest. Even after Carey tied him to a tree and came inside the restaurant, her dog kept barking.

"What is his problem?" Ben asked after Carey carried over her own milk shake and sat with the four kids.

"He's probably barking at somebody on the sidewalk," Carey told him as she took a dainty sip of her treat.

All the kids looked outside. Nobody was there. "I bet he's afraid of his own shadow," Ben said with a laugh.

Carey stood up and glared at Ben. "He's the bravest dog in Bailey City," Carey told Ben before marching out of the restaurant to have a talk with her giant dog.

"Any dog living with a girl like Carey would have to be brave," Annie said.

Kilmer and Annie laughed, but Ben wasn't

even smiling. "Hey," he complained, "some of my milk shake is missing."

"You probably just slurped it faster than you thought," Jane said.

Carey pushed open the door and came back to the table before Ben had a chance to argue. But Carey didn't sit down. She put her hands on her hips and glared at the four kids. "Who's been drinking my milk shake?" she asked.

The kids looked at her cup. Sure enough, half of it was gone. Carey looked right at Ben.

"I didn't do it," Ben said. "There must be a hole in the bottom of your cup."

All of a sudden, Carey's cup emptied with a big slurping sound, but no one was drinking the shake.

Before anyone could stop her, Carey screamed and ran from the restaurant.

6

Big Trouble

"Such a strange girl," Kilmer said as he finished his milk shake. "She's always screaming about something."

"Didn't you notice anything else odd?" Jane asked Kilmer.

Kilmer shrugged. "There are many unusual things about Bailey City," he said before finishing his shake. "But you are the *best* part of Bailey City! Thank you for this wonderful birthday treat!"

"It was our pleasure," Annie said as they threw away their cups and left the restaurant.

"My milk shake was delicious," Annie said, "but it made me even colder."

Ben, Annie, and Jane buttoned their coats against the cool breeze. "Doesn't the wind bother you?" Jane asked Kilmer.

Kilmer shook his head. "Cool breezes make me feel right at home," he explained to his friends. "There are many such drafts at our castle in Transylvania."

The kids made their way down the street. As they walked, Jane noticed more birds squawking and flying from all the trees they passed under.

They hurried past a yard where a black dog growled at them through a fence. "I wonder what's wrong with him today," Ben said. "He usually likes us to stop and play with him."

"Maybe he's too tired to play," Annie suggested. "Dogs get grumpy when they're tired."

Before they reached the end of the block, a gray cat sitting on the sidewalk hunkered down and hissed at them. Then it scrambled up a tree.

"Kilmer's heavy shoes must be scary to little kitty cats," Annie whispered to Jane.

Kilmer did wear heavy shoes, and his footsteps were more like stomps. But Jane

wasn't so sure that's what had frightened the cat.

"Kilmer, I just remembered," Jane blurted. "I haven't seen your cat, Sparky, lately. Is she sick?"

Kilmer's cat always hung around Hauntly Manor Inn, but she wasn't the kind of cat you wanted to pet. She was too busy hissing and trying to scratch.

"Sparky is fine. She just isn't very fond of my great-grandfather," Kilmer explained.

"She stays out of his way whenever he floats in for a visit."

Kilmer walked ahead of his friends while Jane grabbed Annie's arm.

"What's the matter?" Annie asked Jane. "You look like you just saw a ghost."

Annie was right. The color had drained from Jane's face and her lips trembled.

Jane gulped. "Maybe I did!" she said. "Maybe we *all* did."

"Don't be silly," Ben said. "You just drank your milk shake too fast. There's nothing wrong with you that a good game of soccer won't cure." Ben ran to catch up with Kilmer.

But when they turned a corner, Jane saw something that made her scream. At the far end of the street Officer Kelly was riding his horse, and he was headed straight for them.

Jane grabbed Kilmer and twirled him around. "We can't go this way," she warned everybody. "If we do, we'll be in trouble. *Big* trouble!"

7
Animal Catastrophe

"Hurry," Jane said. "Follow me." She reached out and grabbed Kilmer's shirtsleeve, pulling him down a side street. Annie and Ben followed.

"What's wrong with you?" Annie asked as Jane hid behind a bush.

"Shhh," Jane warned, peeking through the branches. "We can't let him hear us."

"Who?" Ben asked.

Jane put her finger to her lips to silence him. The clomping of horse hooves came closer and closer. "Oh, no," she groaned as Officer Kelly and his huge black horse turned down the side street where they hid.

"Run," Jane screamed and dragged her friends down another street. This time she didn't stop to see if Officer Kelly was fol-

lowing them. She rushed down the street and then turned down a tiny alley.

"Why are you running?" Kilmer asked.

"We can't let Officer Kelly see us," Jane gasped as she led her friends around a corner.

"Have you done something wrong?" Annie panted, trying to keep up with her friend.

Jane didn't answer. She glanced over her shoulder to see if Officer Kelly was in sight before pulling her friends down another alley.

"This is great," Ben said and grinned. "Jane is on the run from the law."

"Being a fugitive from the law is not great," Annie warned Jane. "You better tell us what you did."

"I didn't do anything," Jane said as she slowed down, "except save our lives!"

"How did running through the alleys of Bailey City save our lives?" Kilmer asked.

Jane pointed to the roof of Hauntly Manor Inn. "I got us all back to Dedman Street," Jane said as she led them out of the alley and right onto their street. "That's how."

Kilmer shrugged and smiled at Jane. "Very odd," he said. "I didn't realize running down alleys was considered the safest way to get home. Thank you for being such a good friend and showing me." Kilmer waved at his friends and headed for home, leaving Ben and Annie glaring at Jane.

"That was crazy," Ben said as he unbuttoned his coat. "We ran so far I worked up a sweat."

"You're not hot because we ran," Jane told him. "You're hot because the cold breeze is gone."

"That's right," Annie said, unbuttoning her coat. The wind had stopped blowing, but heavy gray storm clouds hung low in the sky. Thunder rumbled in the distance.

"Well, thanks to you, we probably missed all the best television shows," Ben griped. "And we can't play soccer since a storm is about to bombard Bailey City."

"You did make us go the long way to get home," Annie told Jane. "Why were you running from Officer Kelly? He's always nice and lets us pet his horse."

Jane looked around to make sure no one was listening. Then she licked her finger and held it up, testing the wind. "We couldn't let Officer Kelly's horse run into Kilmer's great-grandfather," she told her friends after she was sure there was no more wind.

"Are you crazy?" Ben asked. "I haven't seen Franklin since we left the conservatory."

"Exactly," Jane said. "But he was with us."

"What are you talking about?" Annie asked.

Jane pulled her two friends close. Even though nobody was in sight, she whispered. "Kilmer's great-grandfather is a ghost, and he's haunting Bailey City!"

Ben slapped his forehead and groaned. "Don't start up with your ghost story again," he begged. "You'll ruin a perfectly good afternoon."

"You have to listen to me," Jane warned. "That breeze we felt on the way to Burger Doodle was Franklin."

Annie patted Jane on the shoulder. "That breeze was just part of this storm," Annie told Jane. A loud clap of thunder shook the ground as if to prove Annie's point.

"You're wrong," Jane said. "It was the same draft we felt inside Hauntly Manor Inn when we heard those mysterious footsteps. Franklin followed us so he could taste Doodlegum Shakes. He was the reason the milk shakes disappeared! But having a ghost in Bailey City is worse than disappearing Doodlegum Shakes!"

"Nothing is worse than disappearing milk shakes," Ben argued.

Jane shook her head. "Haven't you noticed all the animals in Bailey City acting berserk?" she asked them.

Annie thought a minute. "That dog was growling at us," she remembered. "And the cat was hissing."

"That's because they don't like ghosts,"

Jane explained. "Even Kilmer admitted that Sparky doesn't like his great-grandfather."

"So what does any of this have to do with acting like a bank robber?" Ben asked.

A huge bolt of lightning arched across the sky. Jane waited for the thunder to stop rumbling before answering.

"Because," Jane told him, "if we had walked past Officer Kelly's horse, there could have been a disaster. We have to do something about Franklin, before we have an animal catastrophe in Bailey City!"

8

Birthday Surprise

Rain sent the kids running for the nearest porch, the one at Hauntly Manor Inn. "Oh, no," Ben groaned. "Here comes trouble."

Carey raced up onto the porch with her dog Chewy. "Why did it have to rain?" Carey complained. "Now my hair is a mess."

"It looks fine," Annie said nicely, even though Carey's curly hair was sticking up in funny directions.

Ben snickered. "Yeah, it's fine, if you're a witch."

Carey started to fuss at Ben, but a large clap of thunder made them jump. Fat raindrops splattered to the ground. "Let's make a deal," Jane suggested. "We'll all try to get along until this storm passes."

40

"I always get along," Ben said as the front door of Hauntly Manor Inn squeaked open.

"Please come inside out of the storm," Kilmer invited the kids.

"Thank you," Carey said, pushing past the other kids. "This weather is terrible on my hair. It's very soft, you know."

Ben rolled his eyes and muttered, "Soft, like your head."

Kilmer clapped his hands. "Now you can share my birthday surprise with me."

"What's the surprise?" Annie asked.

Kilmer shrugged. "If I knew what it was, it wouldn't be a surprise."

The minute the kids were inside the cob-webbed hallway of Hauntly Manor, Chewy started whining. Annie whined, too, when a big bolt of lightning flashed across the sky and thunder boomed above their heads.

Kilmer smiled. "I just love lightning. It makes me feel so alive!"

Another flash of lightning made Chewy howl, and with a crackle, the electricity went out. The kids were left in total darkness.

"Oh, my gosh," Jane said, staring into the darkness. "What's that sound?"

"Someone is playing an organ," Annie said nervously.

The kids listened as eerie music filled the hallway. Chewy howled along with the haunting melody.

"What is going on around here?" Carey demanded. "No lights and weird music. What kind of hotel is this anyway?"

"It sounds like the music is coming from the attic," Ben said, ignoring Carey and tilting his ear toward the ceiling.

"That is surprising," Kilmer told them. "We've never even been in the attic since we've moved here."

"Why not?" Jane said. "I think an attic would be fun to explore."

"Let's go check it out," Ben suggested.

Annie gasped. "Are you crazy? Let's wait until the lights come back on."

"That may be too late," Ben said. "We have to go now."

9
The Attic

"I'm not going anywhere until the lights come back on," Annie said firmly.

Kilmer clomped down the hall. "I have an idea," he said over his shoulder. In three minutes he reappeared carrying two huge candelabras, aglow with lit candles.

"Thank goodness," Carey said with relief. "I'm glad to have some light, but don't you have a flashlight around here somewhere?"

"Flashlight?" Kilmer asked, like he'd never heard of such a thing.

"Forget flashlights," Ben snapped as he grabbed one of the candelabras. "Let's find out what's making that creepy music."

Kilmer led the way up the huge wooden staircase. His shadow loomed on the wall in front of him. It was huge and menacing.

In fact, the candles made strange shadows all around them. Annie would have closed her eyes, if she hadn't been afraid of falling down the stairs.

The organ music got louder and louder, until finally Kilmer stopped and pointed to a door. "There's the attic," he said.

Suddenly the music stopped and Chewy growled. The hair on the back of Chewy's neck stood up, and he bared his teeth.

Annie gulped. "If Chewy is afraid, then we should be, too."

"Don't be silly," Ben told her. "Chewy's been around Carey so long, he's afraid of his own shadow."

Carey glared at Ben.

"I wonder if my great-grandfather is in the attic," Kilmer said.

"You're not afraid of an itty-bitty attic are you?" Carey said.

Kilmer shrugged. "Yes, I am."

"If Kilmer is afraid," Jane whispered to Annie, "then we're in big trouble."

"I am frightened. My great-grandfather

doesn't get along well with dogs," Kilmer explained.

Ben pointed to the attic door impatiently. "Let's not stare at the door all day. Let's go in."

Kilmer pulled on the door handle as thunder rumbled in the distance and a cool draft filled the stairway. The wind snapped the life out of the candles and Chewy bolted up the steps.

"Great-grandfather!" Kilmer screamed as Chewy leaped into the attic.

10

Dust Bunnies

As soon as Chewy disappeared up the attic steps, the organ music stopped. Hauntly Manor Inn grew deathly silent. A jagged bolt of lighting flashed in the stairway window, casting the kids in eerie light. The following thunder seemed even louder without the organ playing.

"Come back, Chewy!" Carey called.

Instead of hearing Chewy galloping back down the steps, something clanked onto the attic floor above the kids' heads.

"W-wh-what's that?" Ben stammered.

"Very odd," Kilmer said matter-of-factly. "I've never heard sounds like that."

Annie grabbed Jane. "We have to get out of here," she whimpered.

"We can't leave without my dog," Carey

snapped. "Besides, with Chewy here we have nothing to worry about. He'll protect us."

"Protect us from what?" Annie asked nervously.

"From whatever is in that attic," Carey said firmly.

"Don't be so sure," Jane warned. "Chewy may be no match for what's in the Hauntlys' attic."

"Besides, I'm sure there's nothing in that attic except spiderwebs and dust bunnies," Carey said with a huff.

"I don't think dust bunnies make that kind of noise," Jane pointed out as loud thumps made their way across the attic. It sounded like something heavy was being dragged across the floor. Chewy started barking again. There was a good dose of growling mixed in.

"That's only thunder," Carey said, but she didn't sound very sure. She pushed past Annie and Jane. "I'm going after my dog. You'll come with me," she said, "unless you're too scared."

Ben puffed out his chest. "I'm not afraid of anything," he blurted. "I'll go with you."

Jane nodded. "We should all stick together," she said. "Just in case."

Kilmer stepped up to Carey. "We must find your dog," he said, "before Chewy finds my great-grandfather!"

"Of course," Carey said proudly, "your great-grandfather would be afraid of a great dog like Chewy."

Kilmer looked at Carey and shook his head. "It's your dog I am worried about," he said. "Not my great-grandfather!"

The door to the attic loomed before them like a black hole leading into a cave. The kids groped their way along the wall as they slowly climbed the steps. Their only light was an occasional streak of lightning.

Jane brushed away cobwebs and Annie was sure she heard something scurrying at her feet. Chewy's barking and growling sounded like a monster lurked in the attic.

"I think Chewy has something cor-

nered," Carey told Kilmer. "He's a great guard dog!"

Finally, they reached the top step. The five kids huddled at the top of the attic stairs. The only light filtered through a dirty window at the far end of the attic, but it was enough for them to see Carey's dog, and he was attacking something.

Annie covered her eyes. "Is that Kilmer's great-grandfather?"

"We need more light," Ben hollered.

"Quick, try the switch," Jane suggested. "Maybe the electricity is back on by now."

Kilmer reached up and grabbed a long chain connected to a lightbulb in the ceiling. He pulled the chain and a tiny beam of light lit up the dingy attic.

11

The End of the Hauntlys

"I don't believe it," Jane said.

Kilmer smiled and Annie giggled. Ben laughed out loud. "Carey's dog caught something, all right," he said between giggles.

Chewy stopped growling and looked at the kids. In his mouth was a huge pair of red-and-white polka-dotted boxer shorts. Carey's face turned as red as the underwear her dog was chewing.

"I do believe we have exposed Chewy's brief career as the greatest of all underwear guard dogs!" Ben said and broke into another fit of giggles.

Carey put her hands on her hips. "You stop that right now," she warned Ben. "My dog does not attack underwear unless there is a reason."

"Carey could be right," Jane interrupted

"Carey could be right," Jane interrupted before Ben could make another joke.

"Carey is never right," Ben argued, but Jane ignored him.

"Could those belong to your great-grand-father?" Jane asked Kilmer, pointing to the boxer shorts that were now draped over Chewy's big head.

Kilmer shrugged his big shoulders. "I have never seen my great-grandfather's underwear," he admitted. He walked closer to Chewy to get a better look.

When he did, Jane pulled Annie and Ben to her. Carey leaned in close to eavesdrop. "I think Chewy thought he was attacking a ghost," Jane told Ben and Annie.

"Why would a ghost need underwear?" Annie asked.

Carey pushed into the kids' huddle. "What is all this talk about underwear and ghosts? There are no such things as ghosts!"

"But if there were, this would be the perfect attic for them to haunt," Annie pointed out.

For the first time, the kids glanced at the Hauntlys' attic. Cobwebs draped all the corners and dust covered every square inch. A rusted suit of armor stood nearby, and wooden crates were piled everywhere. A moldy blanket covered something big in the far corner.

"This is a crummy attic," Carey snapped as she pulled the boxer shorts off Chewy's head and threw them on top of a warped trunk. "My attic is filled with toys and the walls are painted with a giant rainbow. But this attic has nothing interesting at all!"

"A knight's armor is interesting," Annie said, thumping the suit with her hand.

Ben marched across the attic and pulled the blanket to the floor. Underneath it was a giant organ. "This must've been where the music came from," Ben said. "An organ in an attic is interesting, too."

"I wonder what's in this trunk," Jane said

as she pushed the chewed-up underwear to the floor. Kilmer, Ben, and Annie crowded around the open trunk. Carey tried to peek over their shoulders.

The trunk was filled with musty clothes and books. On top of them all were yellowed articles torn from a newspaper. "These are all about the sinking of the *Titanic*," Jane whispered.

"Let me see those," Carey demanded and pushed Kilmer aside. She grabbed the papers and leafed through them. Then she let them flutter to the floor. "Who cares about an old leaky ship at the bottom of the ocean?" she asked.

Jane glanced down at the papers on the floor and gasped. She quickly grabbed the one that had fallen on top of Carey's shoe. "Does this man look familiar to you?" she asked Kilmer.

Kilmer studied the picture and nodded. "Of course. He looks just like my great-grandfather," he said.

"Maybe it *is* Kilmer's great-grandfather," Annie said.

"Don't be ridiculous," Carey said. "It says right there in the article that the man in the picture died on the *Titanic*."

"Exactly," Jane said.

"Are you trying to tell me that I'm standing in a house that is haunted by the ghost of Kilmer's great-grandfather?" Carey squealed.

Nobody said a word. Not even Kilmer. Carey gasped. Her face turned a sickly shade of green. Then she screamed. "Wait until I tell my father!" Carey warned as she grabbed Chewy's collar and headed for the stairs. "This will be the end of the Hauntlys forever!"

Just then a blast from the organ made Carey freeze.

12

Batty Birthday

Annie, Ben, Carey, and Jane dove behind the open trunk. Only Kilmer stayed to face the music. "Kilmer, get back here," Ben shouted over the organ music.

Kilmer shook his head and smiled. "Listen, I know that song."

"It's the death march!" Carey shrieked. "Someone get me out of this madhouse!"

"Hey, I know that song, too," Annie said, lifting her head up over the trunk. "It's the birthday song."

The other three kids popped their heads up and listened. The music was slow and haunting, but there was no denying the familiar tune.

"Great-grandfather!" Kilmer shouted. Kilmer's great-grandfather sat at the dusty organ playing the birthday song. He was wearing a white tuxedo with tails that hung down over the organ stool. With his white hair and white suit, he looked like a ghost to Annie.

"We're in an attic with a ghost," Annie whimpered to Jane.

Before Jane could answer, the door to the attic burst open and a bat flew in. Actually, it was a bat cake carried in by Boris and Hilda.

"Surprise!" Boris, Hilda, and Franklin shouted together. "Happy Birthday!"

Franklin whirled around on the organ stool. "Did you like our Happy *Boo* Day Surprise?" he asked.

Kilmer hugged his great-grandfather. "Of course, I'm so glad you could be here for my birthday surprise."

"What a strange family," Carey mumbled under her breath.

Ben laughed. "How come I never get a birthday surprise like this?"

The kids sang to Kilmer and helped him blow out the candles on his bat cake. They

helped him eat the delicious devil's food bat cake. "Yum," Carey said. "I want this cake for my birthday, too."

Ben licked his fingers. "I can't believe Carey actually likes something about the Hauntlys."

"Shhh," Annie whispered.

"That's right," Jane said softly. "We don't want her remembering about ghosts at Hauntly Manor Inn."

Boris offered the kids another piece of cake. "Does anyone want any rattlesnake punch?" he asked.

Carey and Kilmer sipped the red liquid, but Annie, Jane, and Ben politely refused.

"Hey!" Jane said as she looked around. "What happened to Franklin?"

"He was here a second ago," Ben said, glancing around the attic.

Annie gulped. "It's like he just disappeared."

"Great-grandfather had some other surprise visits to make. He usually disappears quite suddenly. But I'm so glad you could

all be here for my birthday surprise." Kilmer licked the black icing from his lips and asked for more cake.

Annie breathed a sigh of relief. "Well, I guess that means things are back to normal on Dedman Street."

Jane shook her head. "As long as the Hauntlys live here, you never know what the next surprise might be!"

About the Authors

Marcia Thornton Jones and Debbie Dadey like to write about monsters. Their first series with Scholastic, **The Adventures of the Bailey School Kids,** has many characters who are *monsterously* funny. Now with the Hauntly family, Marcia and Debbie are in monster heaven!

Marcia and Debbie both used to live in Lexington, Kentucky. They were teachers at the same elementary school. When Debbie moved to Aurora, Illinois, she and Marcia had to change how they worked together. These authors now create monster books long-distance. They play hot potato with their stories, passing them back and forth by computer.

About the Illustrator

John Steven Gurney is the illustrator of both **The Bailey City Monsters** and **The Adventures of the Bailey School Kids.** He uses real people in his own neighborhood as models when he draws the characters in Bailey City. John has illustrated many books for young readers. He lives in Vermont with his wife and two children.

Creepy, weird, wacky, and funny things happen to the Bailey School Kids!™ Collect and read them all!

The Adventures of THE BAILEY SCHOOL KIDS

Available wherever you buy books, or use this order form

Scholastic Inc., P.O. Box 7502, Jefferson City, MO 65102

Please send me the books I have checked above. I am enclosing \$_____ (please add \$2.00 to cover shipping and handling). Send check or money order — no cash or C.O.D.s please.

Name _____

Address _____

City_____ State/Zip _____

Please allow four to six weeks for delivery. Offer good in the U.S. only. Sorry, mail orders are not available to residents of Canada. Prices subject to change.   BSK1098

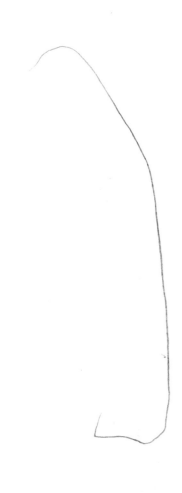